Praise for *Julius Zebra: Rumble with the Romans*

"SOMETIMES A BOOK COMES ALONG THAT IS **PURE JOY,** AND THIS IS ONE OF THEM"
LITERARY REVIEW

"AS WELL AS PROVIDING **MUCH HILARITY** *JULIUS ZEBRA* CUNNINGLY EDUCATES ABOUT ANCIENT ROME WITHOUT EVER FEELING LIKE A LESSON … **HIGHLY RECOMMENDED"**
THE SCHOOL LIBRARIAN

"THE **COMICALLY CLASSICAL** WAY TO LEARN ABOUT THE ROMANS!"
LANCASHIRE EVENING POST

"THE BOOK HAS A VERY *HORRIBLE HISTORIES* SENSE OF HUMOUR AND GROUNDS ITS **SILLINESS** WITH FACTS ABOUT GLADIATORIAL COMBAT"
FINANCIAL TIMES

"*MADAGASCAR* MEETS *GLADIATOR* IN THIS EXCITING, ACTION-PACKED AND **HYSTERICALLY FUNNY** STORY BRIMMING WITH ENTERTAINING ROMAN FACTS"
WORLD BOOK DAY

"**BONKERS BUT BRILLIANT"**
ANGELS & URCHINS

"HAS A **LAUGH OUT LOUD** CARTOON ON NEARLY EVERY PAGE"
THE HERALD

"THIS IS *HORRIBLE HISTORIES, MAMMAL STYLE"*
INIS

"COMPLETELY **RIDICULOUS** PLOT LINE AND ZANY CHARACTERS ARE HIGHLY ENTERTAINING AND SOMEHOW MANAGE TO COMBINE DAFT ANTICS WITH HISTORICAL FACTS. **GREAT!"**
WRD MAGAZINE

"THERE ARE PLENTY OF SNIPPETS OF HISTORY TO BE PICKED UP WHILE ENJOYING THE STORY"
PARENTS IN TOUCH

"BEHOLD A **BONKERS** BLAST-FROM-THE-PAST, FILLED WITH MAYHEM AND HISTORICAL FACTS. YOUNG READERS WILL BE MESMERISED"
LITTLE LONDON

GARY NORTHFIELD

WALKER
BOOKS

For my wonderful friend
and studio-mate, Sarah McIntyre

Special thanks as always to Lizzie & Jack,
and to Lucy, for their editorial and designer
skillz and their deep reserves of patience

First published in Great Britain 2016 by Walker Books Ltd
87 Vauxhall Walk, London SE11 5HJ

2 4 6 8 10 9 7 5 3 1

© 2016 Gary Northfield

The right of Gary Northfield to be identified as author and illustrator
of this work has been asserted by him in accordance with the
Copyright, Designs and Patents Act 1988

This book has been typeset in Stempel Schneidler

Printed and bound in Great Britain by Clays Ltd, St Ives plc

British Library Cataloguing in Publication Data:
a catalogue record for this book is available from the British Library

ISBN 978-1-4063-5493-5

www.walker.co.uk

CONTENTS

So, you think you know about

JULIUS
ZEBRA?

Julius wasn't quite like other zebras. Not only did he live during ROMAN TIMES, but he was also the

PEOPLE'S CHAMPION!!

EXCITING, RIGHT?

{CHAPTER ONE}
THE PEOPLE'S CHAMPION

Walking through the noisy, smelly, bustling streets of Rome, Julius felt as if he was Caesar himself! The place may have smelled worse than a gnu's bottom, much like the stinky lake back home, but out here, unlike back home, everybody LOVED him.

Since his triumphant, surprise victory at Rome's greatest amphitheatre, the Colosseum, only a month ago, Julius had been transformed into a GLADIATOR SUPERSTAR!

Stories of his deeds had spread like wildfire throughout the vast Empire. People were coming from all over just to see Julius fight and he was loving every minute of it.

Scuttling next to Julius was his friend Cornelius the warthog. Cornelius was a tiny little chap and in the mêlée of the crowded street he had to fight hard not to be trodden on.

"Stop panicking, Cornelius!" said Julius as he merrily waved to his fans. "We have PLENTY of time. Let the people of Rome enjoy the treat of seeing their hero walking among them!"

Cornelius tutted. "Careful, soon your head might get too big to walk down these narrow streets."

Suddenly, a scruffy young girl approached Julius, holding out a tatty parchment.

Julius ruffled the little girl's hair. "Of course, my dear little thing – do you have any ink?"

The girl pulled a very sad face. "No..." she sighed.

Julius quickly looked around the street to see what he could use to make a print. "How about if I dipped my hoof in mud? You'd have your very own Julius Zebra muddy hoofprint!"

The little girl's face lit up. "Oh yes please, Mr Zebra, that would be wonderful! Thank you!"

Julius bent down and squished his front right hoof into the mud, then he placed it very carefully onto the girl's parchment. He pulled his hoof away to reveal a perfect print.

"THAT IS SO AMAZING!!! THANK YOU MR
ZEBRA!!!" squeaked the girl. "I LOVE YOU!!!"
She kissed the print and ran off to a group of her
friends who were standing nearby, who all squealed
like little mice and jumped for joy at seeing such an
exciting souvenir.

Julius sniffed his hoof, screwing up his nostrils.
"You know, I don't think that actually was mud."

He passed his hoof
to Cornelius to sniff.

"Quick!" said Cornelius. "Let's run the other way, we'll be long gone before she notices." And they scooted off into the crowds.

"WAIT!" cried a voice. "WHERE ARE YOU GOING?! WAIT FOR ME!" From one of the many shops that lined the street came bounding a lively antelope clutching a lump of rock.

"Let me guess, Felix," said Julius. "Is it a rock?"

"Well!" said Felix proudly. "What you have here is an actual piece of the PYRAMID OF GIZA IN EGYPT!!!"

Cornelius examined the rock carefully. "The only 'Giza' this rock has seen is the dodgy geezer who sold you this worthless rubbish!" he huffed. "These Roman shopkeepers see you coming a mile away, Felix. I don't know why you keep buying these stupid rocks."

"Forget all that," said Julius. "Where are the others? We promised to meet them here at noon!"

"Yes!" agreed Cornelius. "As I keep saying, we need to be heading back to the Colosseum. Julius has his important fight this afternoon in front of the Emperor to celebrate the Festival of Quinquatria!"

"The Festival of *Quinquatria!*" corrected
Cornelius. "It is a festival in honour of Minerva.
She's the goddess of wisdom, so it's hardly
surprising you've never heard of her."

"Well, how RUDE!" snorted Felix.

Julius put his arms round his friends. "Stop
it now, you two!" he laughed. "Don't forget,
Emperor Hadrian has finally PROMISED us our
FREEDOM if I win this fight!"

"JULIUS!" cried a voice in the crowd. "JULIUS,
WAIT!"

Julius turned round, expecting to greet one of his many fans, but was instead faced with the beaming sharp teeth of a smiling crocodile.

"LUCIA!" said Julius, pleased to see his friend. "How was the chariot racing?"

"A-MA-ZING!!!" she said.

"Rufus found you a present, too!" she squealed.

"He did?" asked Julius excitedly, clapping his hooves. A long shadow loomed over Julius, who looked up to see his friend, Rufus the giraffe.

"I did!" replied Rufus, and he handed a tiny statuette to the eager zebra.

"We didn't realise how popular you REALLY are!" said Lucia. "Look! It's a figurine of YOU!"

"That's BRILLIANT!" laughed Felix. "It even has your mad bog-eyes!"

Julius fired a dirty look towards Felix. "WHAT mad bog eyes?!"

Rufus quickly interjected to save the poor antelope. "They had a big stall selling hundreds of them! You are PROPER famous now!"

As if on cue, an excited mob started to crowd around the animals as people clamoured to see the gladiator superstar who was actually walking down their street.

"Come on!" said Cornelius. "We really should head back to the school before this lot tear us apart."

They pushed past the frenzied crowd out onto the main road that ran through the heart of Rome. Dashing under the arches of the great aqueduct and past the grand palace that sat up on the hill, the animals headed for the huge stone stadium that loomed large on the horizon.

They raced past the crowds that were massing around the Colosseum and dashed RIGHT past the Colosseum itself.

Instead, they ran into an unassuming square building next to the amphitheatre, past the gruff guards at the door and into a huge courtyard that housed its own mini arena.

This was Ludus Magnus, Rome's biggest and best gladiator school and home to Julius and his pals. The *click-clack* of wooden swords could be heard as gladiators honed their fighting skills, but there was no time to stand and watch. They raced downstairs towards the tunnel that led directly to the underbelly of the Colosseum, only to find their way blocked by a scrawny, surly lion.

"Sorry, Milus!" gasped Julius, catching his breath. "But we had terrible trouble trying to outmanoeuvre my hordes of fans!"

Their grouchy companion just tutted and stepped to one side. "You have a hard life, zebra," he growled sarcastically. "Anyway, it's not me you've got to apologise to, it's PLINY!"

Julius slapped his forehead with his hoof. "Oh no! I promised Pliny I'd meet him early to brush up on those new sword moves he's been teaching me."

He sprinted down the tunnel, the stench of the rancid dungeons hitting his nose as he ran. He careered around a corner, past the cages with the growling leopards and towards one of the many lifts that spirited animals up into the arena.

The little mouse threw a gold helmet at Julius.

"You'd better get yourself suited and booted!" he said. "If you're ever gonna make a good impression in front of Hadrian, then today has to be the day!"

"Ah, you don't need no extra training!" laughed
Pliny. "Your opponent is as useless as ALL the
other animals you've had to face." The little mouse
gave Julius a friendly punch on his shin. "There
ain't no animal gladiator like YOU, Debra!"

"It's ZEBRA, not Debra!" said Julius, rolling his
eyes. "How many times?"

"Zebra, Debra, Martha! Whatevah!" replied
Pliny, pushing Julius into his cage.

CHAPTER TWO
ZEBRAMANIA!

Julius's heart pounded as the cage lifted up towards the ceiling, scraping roughly against the stone walls. Over the creaking of the stiff wooden frames, Julius could clearly make out the chanting of the crowd. "ZEBRA! ZEBRA! ZEBRA!"

The cage stopped moving with a great THUMP and Julius had to grab the wooden bars to stop himself falling over.

Just above him he could hear the voice of the Summa Rudis, the referee.

"CITIZENS OF ROME!" bellowed the Summa Rudis. "As you all know, to celebrate the Festival of Quinquatria, Emperor Hadrian has decreed that you should enjoy a day of FEASTING and FIGHTING!" The crowd roared. "YOUR FIRST OPPONENT," he screamed, "Rome's very own PEOPLE'S CHAMPION, JULIUS ZEBRA!!"

Ahead of Julius a trapdoor opened to a thunderous cheer and the blast of a hundred trumpets. He bounded through the hatchway.

Julius threw up his arms to greet the 80,000-strong crowd, who were roaring his name so loudly that the whole amphitheatre shook.

Eager to show off his skills, Julius leapt into a backwards somersault, throwing his sword into the air and deftly catching it while landing nimbly on the arena floor like a cat. The spellbound audience erupted into another round of chanting and cheering.

Watching from the sidelines, Julius's proud friends were on their feet, clapping and cheering him along.

Over on the other side of the arena in his gold and marble royal box sat the Emperor Hadrian, enthusiastically applauding his zebra champion.

Excellent! thought Julius. *Hadrian seems to be in a good mood. There's no way he's not granting me my freedom today!*

In the centre of the arena stood the Summa Rudis, a beefy man wearing a white tunic embellished with two long blue parallel stripes. In his right hand he held up a big stick.

The Summa Rudis battled to make himself heard.
"YOUR SECOND OPPONENT!" he screamed.
"ALL THE WAY FROM THE CITY OF ALEXANDRIA
IN EGYPT, the mighty camel warrior, IMHOTEP!"

From the gates a hapless camel came stumbling in,
his loose, ill-fitting armour rattling as he scrambled
across the arena floor. As he reached the Summa
Rudis, he clumsily tripped over his spear and landed
in a clattering heap on the floor.

The crowd roared with laughter.

On the sidelines, Milus shook his head in despair. "Where do they find these idiots?"

Julius took up his position in the arena and smacked his sword noisily into his shield with a dramatic growl. This threw the crowd into another wild frenzy. Imhotep the camel gulped and took a small step backwards. He nervously glanced over his shoulder as the zebra-mad spectators hurled insults and rotten food in his direction.

The horns of the cornicen trumpeted the start of the fight and the Summa Rudis stepped aside. The Colosseum roared.

Julius edged confidently towards the twitchy Egyptian camel, flicking his sword from behind his shield.

"'AVE 'IM!" yelled the crowd. "LOP HIS HEAD OFF! FINISH HIM!"

Imhotep timidly shuffled backwards, his armour jangling as he shivered with fear. "Come on!" cried Julius. "At least try to hit me with your spear, give the punters a bit of a show. I promise I won't hurt you too much!" The camel gulped and shook his head. Rotten vegetables splattered his nice shiny headdress. The audience screamed.

Imhotep finally collapsed onto the floor, sobbing. "PLEASE DON'T KILL ME, ZEBRA!" he cried. "DON'T BLOW ME UP WITH MAGIC LIGHTNING FROM YOUR EYES!"

Julius stood over the blubbing Egyptian and kicked his spear away with his hoof. "I shall spare your life, Imhotep," he declared. "No lightning shall pass from my eyes today."

"Come now," said Julius, turning to the crowd. "You want I should give this camel the HUMP?"

Pliny turned to Milus. "Please tell me he didn't really just say that?"

"I'm afraid he did," replied Milus flatly.

In the arena, the Summa Rudis grabbed Julius's arm and thrust it into the air. "THE WINNER!" he announced.

Julius jumped for joy and excitedly turned to the royal box to seek the Emperor's approval and his long-awaited promise of freedom.

But the royal box was empty. Hadrian was gone!

Julius's friends suddenly came dashing across the arena.

"Milus saw him receive a message, then he stormed off in a huff!"

Julius flopped to the floor in despair. "But, he PROMISED...!" he sobbed.

Felix tried to console him. "If it helps, Hadrian didn't look happy to leave, he was really enjoying himself until he scarpered..."

Julius looked like he was ready to burst into tears. "We'll NEVER win our freedom!" he whimpered. "We'll be stuck in this Roman poohole for the REST OF OUR LIVES!"

As Julius dragged himself up and began to shuffle miserably out of the arena, a familiar figure stood in his way. "Then you'll be pleased to hear my news, donkey!" came a gruff voice.

"Septimus," groaned Julius.

The towering figure of the Lanista, boss of the gladiator school, stood in front of them, hands on his hips.

"OOH! A SURPRISE!" squealed Julius, clapping his hooves. "I LOVE surprises!"

"He wants to see you all in the school arena at sunrise," growled Septimus. "And make sure your knapsacks are packed. You're going on a nice long trip!"

Julius and the others were beside themselves with glee. "A LONG TRIP?!" cried Julius. "WE'RE GOING ON OUR HOLIBOBS!!"

We're going on our holibobs. Tra la la la!!

"I wouldn't trust these scoundrels as far as I could throw them," Milus growled. "The only trip we're going on is to the forests of Germania to face the BARBARIAN HORDE!"

⚜CHAPTER THREE⚜
ROMAN HOLIDAY!

At the first crow of the cockerel the next morning, Julius sprang out of bed.

All the animals quickly got dressed, ate their bowls of porridge and dashed down to the small arena in the centre of the school.

Septimus strode in, clapping his hands bossily. "LINE UP IN THE CENTRE YOU 'ORRIBLE LOT! QUICKLY! QUICKLY!"

Septimus could barely BELIEVE HIS EYES!

"BY THE FIERY BEARD OF JUPITER, WHAT DO YOU THINK YOU ARE ALL DOING?!" he bellowed. "I said pack your knapsacks, not dress up as CLOWNS!" He stormed up to Rufus the giraffe, snatched his fishing rod from his hoof and snapped it in two over his knee.

"I ought to send you all straight to the galleys as punishment!" he yelled.

Septimus leaned in to Cornelius's face. "It's not FUN, warthog, it's HORRIBLE!"

"Forget that!" cried Felix. "Tell us about this brilliant holiday! Will there be pebble beaches?"

Milus the lion grabbed Septimus by his tunic and pulled him up to his big teeth. "And please," he snarled, "be sure to explain how it is we're being sent on holiday, as opposed to being *set free...*?"

Suddenly, from the east entrance to the arena, the Emperor Hadrian strode in flanked by elite Roman guards.

I'll explain everything now, lion.

Hadrian?

Milus, not wanting the whole Roman army on top of him, reluctantly dropped Septimus, who harrumphed and readjusted his crumpled tunic.

Hadrian addressed the animals. "Listen to me, beasts: Julius's battle yesterday at the Festival of Quinquatria convinced me that he is one of the greatest champions of Rome." He walked up and down, looking at the animals proudly. "In fact, throughout the Empire you are now ALL legends, heroes that every man and creature aspires to be!"

Hadrian stopped in front of Julius and placed his hand on the zebra's shoulder. "So much so, that I need you, my People's Champions, to go to the distant corner of our Empire and INSPIRE my citizens!" He waved his fist triumphantly in the air. "I want you to show them what it means to be a WARRIOR ROMAN!"

I have arranged a tournament for you all.

Win that and THEN I shall grant you your freedom!

He stared Julius right in his eye. Julius blinked nervously, not knowing where to look.

"Sounds fair enough," he mumbled. "Where are we off to then? Gaul? Egypt? Will I need my bucket and spade?"

"We are sending you to BRITANNIA!" declared Hadrian. All the animals looked at each other bewildered.

"BRITANNIA?!" cried Julius. "Oh, how PERFECT!!"

"Ah." Hadrian smiled, impressed. "You have heard of our exotic little outpost, then?"

"Ooh no, never heard of the place!" replied Julius. "I'm just excited about going on holibobs!"

Cornelius's grin turned into a grimace. "I've heard of it," he whispered to Julius, "and it's not good."

It is a strange and distant land.

Only A FOOL would go there for a holiday.

Milus was also unconvinced. "So, we just turn up, entertain the locals, and then we can go free?"

"Yes!" replied Hadrian. "Something like that."

He turned to Septimus. "Get them ready Septimus, the ship leaves at noon."

"YOU HEARD THE EMPEROR!" Septimus bellowed. "NOW PACK YOUR KIT LIKE REAL WARRIORS AND BE READY FOR NOON!"

Felix put up his hoof. Septimus nearly collapsed in frustration. "WHAT IS IT NOW?!!"

"Um, so *will* we be needing buckets and spades on this trip? Hadrian wasn't very clear."

Felix thought for a moment. "I'm thinking ... 'Yes'?"

Septimus moved his head closer to Felix's face and let out a low growl.

"NO!" squealed Felix. "I mean 'No'!"

Septimus leaned back. "CORRECT answer! Now, get moving. And if I see one single bucket or spade, you'll ALL be on a one-way trip to the battlefields of GERMANIA!"

CHAPTER FOUR

ALL ABOARD!

By midday, everyone was packed and ready to leave. They jumped onto the back of a cart waiting to take them to the port of Ostia.

Julius was so excited that he decided it was time for a jolly singsong to get everyone in the holiday mood.

"Come on everybody, after me! OH, I DO LIKE TO BE BESIDE THE SEASIDE!!"

As the others joined in, Julius noticed that Septimus was having a quiet chat with his champion gladiator, Victorious.

"Those two are ALWAYS whispering to each other!" replied Cornelius. "They're like a couple of old fishwives."

Milus let out a big huff. "Well, I don't like it one bit. In fact," he growled, "I don't like this 'trip' one bit!"

Julius gave the grumpy lion a big ruffle of his tatty mane.

"You ALWAYS see the worst in everything! I'm just desperate to get this holiday started!"

Julius leaned out of the cart and called out to Septimus. "COME ON! I'm sure you'll see each other again! Just give that idiot a big kiss and LET'S GET GOING!"

"ALL RIGHT, ALL RIGHT!" growled Septimus as he stormed to the cart and hopped onto his seat. "Insolent animals! If I had my way, you'd be well on your way to—"

And so, finally, they all sped off to the great Roman port of Ostia, where an hour later they found their ship waiting for them in the dock.

They ran onto the deck and began exploring the impressive vessel and all its nooks and crannies.

"Right, you 'orrible lot!" shouted Septimus as he came on board. "Line up on the deck, NOW!" They all scooted to the middle of the ship, dutifully lining up as instructed. Septimus marched up and down, looking at them very sternly. "This voyage is going to be a VERY LONG voyage and I intend to keep you all busy on this ship."

"CORRECT!" cried Septimus. "I DO mean star jumps. AND scrubbing the deck, plus any other rotten jobs I can think of to keep you out of trouble!"

"BAH!" blurted Milus. "I told you! Some HOLIDAY this is going to be!"

Ignoring the lion, Septimus continued with his lecture. "In fact, we will start with SCRUBBING this filthy deck! Everyone grab a bucket and brush. QUICKLY! I want it so clean and shiny I can see my FACE in it!"

As they all furiously scrubbed away, the ship pulled out of Ostia.

Farewell old friend!

Julius polished the rotten wooden deck as hard as he could, but he was nowhere near getting anything like a shine on it. "This is pointless!" he gasped. "My arms will fall off before we see Septimus's ugly mug on this deck!"

Felix leaned over to Julius. "Milus was right, this is no holiday! This is WORK!" he whispered. "I think I would rather have stayed back in the gladiator school!"

Cornelius shuffled over to join in the grumbling.

Lucia and Rufus sidled across to see what everyone was whispering about.

"Are you all moaning about doing this horrible work?" asked Lucia very quietly, peering over her shoulder to make sure Septimus wasn't looking.

"Yeah, you could say that!" huffed Julius, struggling to keep his voice down.

Felix plopped his brush into the bucket of soapy water and straightened his stiff back. "I'm pretty sure holidays mean going away and having a lovely time," he whispered. "And I can tell you now, I am definitely NOT having a lovely time—"

"In fact," roared Septimus, "you can all give me fifty star jumps as punishment!"

"Oh, WHAT?!" blurted Felix, getting up on his hooves. "Did your mum take you on holiday to army training camps or something? This is RIDICULOUS!"

"Yes she DID actually," replied Septimus, smiling fondly. "Best days of my life." He thumped Felix on his shoulder. "YOU can give me an extra fifty star jumps for trying to be a clever clogs." Then he disappeared towards his cabin.

Finally they all flopped to the floor exhausted. "All I can say," wheezed Julius, "is that this tournament had better be worth it!"

"Fear not, Julius," Cornelius wheezed. "I have seen a sign that our fortunes are favoured by the gods!"

Julius rolled his eyes. *Here we go again!* he thought. *Cornelius and his la-lah superstitions.*

The warthog pointed to the big sail fluttering above them.

Cornelius then pointed to Felix, who had accidentally kicked over his bucket of water. "And see how water has been spilt? To spill water when the winds blows in from the East is a sure sign that Neptune, god of the sea, wishes us well on our voyage!"

"And a sure sign that Felix is a clumsy halfwit," growled Milus.

Suddenly Septimus reappeared on deck.

"UH OH! Look out!" said Julius. "Look busy!"

Septimus paced up and down, scrutinizing the sparkling deck.

"Well?" called out Julius. "How did we do? Can you see your glorious face now?"

Septimus spun round and glared at the cheeky zebra. "All I see, donkey, is a bunch of USELESS LAYABOUTS!"

Septimus marched over to the exhausted animals. "You'll have to do better than this tomorrow, beasts. The Empire won't tolerate a filthy ship."

From a knapsack he tossed small brown biscuits at the animals.

"Here's your dinner. Take these biscuits down to the hold where you'll find your sleeping quarters. I'll see you back on deck AT THE CRACK OF DAWN." And he marched back to his cosy cabin.

Julius and his companions wearily pulled themselves up and headed towards the wooden ladder that led below deck, trailing stale biscuit crumbs behind them.

CHAPTER FIVE
STINK HOLE

As they clambered down the slippery ladder, they found a gloomy, very stinky hold. Julius jumped down the last few steps, only to splash into a big puddle.

He squinted into the murkiness and could just make out piles of broken old jugs and rotted crates from voyages past. As he edged forward, his face was suddenly tangled up in what felt like a massive cobweb.

The others came rushing over to rescue their stricken friend. "Don't panic, Julius!" called Cornelius. "We'll save you!!" But the more they tried to pull Julius free, the more everyone got twisted up in the web.

Suddenly from behind them came a low, growly laugh.

It's not a cobweb, you fools. It's a hammock!

"A hammock? What's one of them?" asked Julius.

"What does it look like?" said Milus, lounging back comfortably. "It's a BED!"

"A BED?" cried Julius, befuddled. "How EXCITING!" He pulled the tatty net off his friends and smoothed it out with his hooves. "Anything's got to be better than those rotten sleeping cells back in Rome!" He laughed as he leapt into the air, expecting to flop onto his strange new bed. But instead he fell right through the threadbare net and straight into the big puddle on the floor.

As he pulled himself up and wiped muddy water off his bottom, Julius let out a big sigh. "I'm not sure I can put up with these travelling conditions."

Cornelius tentatively pulled himself up onto a hammock, which seemed to hold his weight as it swayed with the rocking ship. "Seeing as Hadrian thinks we're all People's Champions, I reckon we're being treated pretty shoddily, don't you agree?"

"I tried to warn you!" said Milus. "These Romans are rotten to the core!"

"But what should we do?" asked Julius. "We're the PEOPLE'S CHAMPIONS! I'm not scrubbing floors for no one!"

Lucia the crocodile suddenly put up her claw. "Do not fear, my friends," she whispered, beckoning them to come closer.

She signalled to Rufus to check if any Romans were listening above deck. The giraffe poked his head up, then gave the all clear. The crocodile gathered everyone into a huddle.

"Before you start," interrupted Cornelius, "just so you know, I'm NOT wearing a stupid moustache." He scratched his nose.

I'm still itching after your last escape plan!

Scratch!
Scratch!

"There'll be no moustaches, I promise," replied Lucia.

"But we *will* be wearing brightly coloured checked trousers again, right?" asked Felix. "I thought I looked PRETTY smart in those fancy pants, last time."

Lucia shook her head. "Sorry Felix, no fancy trousers, either."

Felix let out a big HUFF and kicked a clay pot.

"This is DEFINITELY the worst holiday I've ever been on!" He sprang grumpily into his hammock, which flipped him over and dumped him onto the floor.

"What's the plan then, Lucia?" whispered Julius, rubbing his hooves together with anticipation. "Spill the beans!"

"Check this out!" she said, and from her knapsack she pulled out some very fine chainmail. "Me and Rufus were having a bit of a nose around down here and we found a whole stash of this stuff!"

"Enough? Enough for what?" asked Cornelius, suspiciously. "Are we dressing up as soldiers and FIGHTING our way off the ship?"

"Nope!" said Lucia as she began wrapping herself in the chainmail.

"FISH?!" everyone echoed in unison.

"Yes!" replied Lucia proudly. "This might not look like much at the moment—"

"You can say THAT again," growled Milus.

"—BUT!" she continued, ignoring the lion, "once me and Rufus have finished making the costumes, we'll all dress up as FISH, sneak up on deck and JUMP into the sea!"

Cornelius was not impressed. "This has to be the most RIDICULOUS idea I've *EVER* heard!" He tugged at Lucia's chainmail. "As soon as Septimus or one of the other Romans hears a big splash, they'll look overboard and see us fools swimming about."

"EXACTLY!" chimed in Rufus. "But, they won't see *US* ... they'll see FISH!" He held out his hooves as if he'd just performed the most amazing magic trick.

Lucia looked at the blank faces around the room. "And then we swim away and be FREE!" she added enthusiastically. "Don't you *see*? The chainmail looks like shiny fish scales! It's an AWESOME plan!"

Julius jumped up and had a good look at the chainmail for himself.

Hmmm...

You know what? I actually think this could work.

"It IS pretty shiny and slippery, just like fish scales," he said, holding it up to the light. "Maybe it's worth a shot!" He turned to the others. "Come on! Do you want to be scrubbing mouldy decks and star-jumping all the way to Britannia?"

Everyone shook their heads.

"NO. I just wanted a jolly holibob like they promised," sobbed Felix.

"OK, I'll do it," said Felix. "But only if I can be a halibut."

Julius patted him on his shoulder. "You can be whatever fish you want."

Felix jumped up and punched the air with his hoof. "Then I'm IN!" he roared.

Julius turned to Cornelius. "And you?"

"I'm coming too!" said Milus. "It's a rubbish plan, but I'm not hanging around on this lousy ship."

"Then it's decided!" declared Julius. "We'll help Lucia and Rufus make the costumes and we'll make our escape as soon as the sun rises!"

{CHAPTER SIX}
GONE FISHING

"WAKE UP, YOU LAYABOUTS!" Septimus's voice boomed down the hatch. "TIME TO GET UP AND SCRUB THOSE DECKS!"

Julius rubbed his tired, bleary eyes with his hooves. They'd been up all night making fish costumes and now they had to put their plan into action.

Wakey wakey, everyone. Time to get this show on the road.

"We're going to need a distraction," said Julius. "I'll go up on deck and pretend to scrub. I'll keep Septimus chatting while you all jump in the sea."

"But what about you?" asked Cornelius. "Aren't you coming with us?"

I'll have my costume in my bucket!

"As soon as Septimus and the crew go to look at all you 'fishes', I'll bung this on then dive in after you," said Julius. "Right!" He bundled his fish costume into the bucket. "Are we all ready?"

"Don't forget," said Julius as he climbed the ladder, "wait till I've got Septimus talking before you jump overboard!"

He scampered up the ladder and out onto the deck, whistling innocently as he went. He waltzed over to the far end of the boat and started pretending to scrub the deck.

Septimus stormed over to him. "WHAT'S GOING ON, DONKEY? WHERE ARE THE REST OF THE LAZY BEASTS?"

"That's our cue, lads!" whispered Lucia and they sneaked up the ladder and out onto the deck.

Julius kept Septimus talking to distract him.

Septimus looked furious and bemused. "EH? What are you babbling on about, donkey? I have no time for this nonsense!"

Behind Septimus there was a sudden shrill scream.

"WHAT IN JUPITER'S BEARD...?!" roared Septimus. He dashed to the side of the ship to see a strange mass of figures thrashing about in the water.

"MAN OVERBOARD!" came the cry from the helmsman.

Septimus leaned over for a closer look. "Those *aren't* men! THAT'S A CROCODILE, A WARTHOG A GIRAFFE, A LION AND AN ANTELOPE!"

Hastily dressed up in his fish disguise, Julius flip-flapped to the side of the boat. "Wait! Surely they're FISH!" he cried. "See their shiny scales! Is that … a GIANT HALIBUT…? Best let them go, Septimus!"

Septimus leaned over to get an even better look. "FISH?! You are more of an imbecile than I gave you credit for, donkey!"

Julius shrugged his shoulders. "Oh well, I tried!" And with that he plunged into the sea with his friends.

Unfortunately, as soon as he plopped in, Julius realised that he could barely move.

In fact, the chainmail was dragging him under.

He frantically looked around and saw that all his friends were also struggling to stay afloat. "HELP US SEPTIMUS!" cried Julius. "WE'RE DROWNING!!"

Using boat hooks and fishing nets the animals were hauled back on board with a big wet PLOP. They flapped about on the deck like floundering fish, but they weren't fooling anyone.

"SEND THESE TURBOT BRAINS DOWN TO THE HOLD!" shrieked Septimus. "I'LL DEAL WITH THEM LATER!"

"I'm so sorry. I nearly killed us all off," snivelled Lucia as they were led down the hatchway. "I'll think of a better plan next time, I promise!"

"Forget about it," said Julius, as he pulled off his costume. "It looks like we're going to have to stick it out on this stinking slave ship. But once we reach Britannia, we'll need to make sure we win Hadrian's tournament and our freedom with it."

Then we can have as long a holiday as we want!

"You really do live in a dream world, zebra!" said Milus as he jumped into his hammock. "Hasn't this trip taught you ANYTHING about these Roman scoundrels?" He picked up his knapsack and started to rummage inside it. "The only escape from these wretches is DEATH!"

"Oh, cheery!" said Julius.

Milus suddenly became very agitated and sprang back out of his hammock.

He turned to Julius. "It must have been YOU!" he snarled. "While we were all splashing about in the water, you must have sneaked back here and eaten them!"

"Have you gone CRAZY?" said Julius. "I was distracting Septimus all that time!"

Milus hurled his knapsack to the floor and grabbed Julius by the throat. "Being stuck on a ship heading towards certain death with you NINCOMPOOPS is bad enough," he snarled, "but stealing my BISCUITS is the last straw."

CHAPTER SEVEN

LAND OF HOPE AND GORY

"Three weeks we've been stuck on this rancid ship…" gasped an exhausted Julius, his head hanging over the side. "If I never see another wave again, it will be too soon."

"At least this time we haven't been cramped up in a tiny box," squeaked Cornelius, also hanging his green face over the side of the ship.

Julius let out a deep sigh. "Not only has Septimus got us working day and night, but I've got that INSANE LION thinking I've scoffed his biscuits. Things couldn't be more unbearable!"

Cornelius looked up to the giant square sail, buffeting in the breeze. "Don't worry, Julius. We've had two days of fair wind, so we should reach our destination very soon."

Julius gazed off into the distance. "I don't think I could suffEEUURGH!!!" He retched over the side again. "Sorry… What I meant to say is, I don't think that I could suffer another day of this trip, Cornelius."

And where has your god Neptune been all this time?

Well you're still alive aren't you?

Cornelius plopped himself down on the deck, exhausted. "That Hadrian really is a rotter," he said. "He must have known what a long, treacherous journey this was going to be. I'll never forgive him for pretending it was some jolly day out."

"Don't you worry, Cornelius," puffed Julius as he plonked down next to his friend. "Once we win the tournament, we'll show those Romans who they're dealing with!"

I'm the PEOPLE'S CHAMPION!

"OI! WILL YOU TWO DIMWITS GET BELOW DECK!" boomed a voice from the captain's cabin. "UNLESS OF COURSE YOU ACTUALLY WANT TO BE WASHED OVERBOARD!"

The two seasick animals dragged themselves up and walked slowly back to the hatchway to the lower deck. But, as they started climbing down the ladder, a great roar of "LAND HO!" came from the lookout on the bow of the ship.

They both turned to look. On the far distant horizon, a dark sliver of land began to appear through the mist.

All the other animals rushed up on deck and gaped at the strange new land.

"Exciting, but perhaps *very dangerous*," warned Cornelius. "From what I understand, the local barbarians are extremely fierce and haven't taken too kindly to the Romans taking over their land."

"Yeah!" said Rufus nervously. "I heard some of the crew say that the place is swarming with gruesome monsters, like HEADLESS MEN!"

"Er, I'm not sure about the headless men," said Cornelius, "but there are *definitely* plenty of weird people living on this island."

Lucia became very excited. "Ooh, what fun! Like who? Who lives here?"

"The local inhabitants are called **BRITONS**.

They are a VERY tall
race and amble about
like **GANGLY
MONKEYS**.

They like to roam around **NAKED**
in swamps all day.

They cover their bodies in amazing **INTRICATE PICTURES**, sometimes of animals, to harness their powers.

They are also **VERY FIERCE** because it is so cold and miserable. And when they get cold, they wear the SKINS OF ANIMALS!"

"You know what," said Felix, "if I were to wear any one of you as a skin, it would probably be Julius. You'd make a lovely pair of stripy trousers!"

"Yeah, thanks for that, Felix," said Julius. "Your antlers would also make a lovely hat."

"You leave my antlers out of this!" squealed Felix, putting his hooves up to defend them.

"I think I'm starting to look forward to this tournament!" said Julius. "I wonder what weird local animals we might be up against? I'm guessing they don't have camels or lions in Britannia."

"The only thing I'm looking forward to," growled Milus, "is finding out who ate my BISCUITS!"

"Oh, will you shut up about your STUPID biscuits!" tutted Julius.

CHAPTER EIGHT
BRITON ROCK

CVII

Julius and the other animals stood shivering on the deck as the ship drifted through the frozen mist. The grey-brown landscape with its scattering of skeletal trees loomed silently as they pulled into the dock.

Julius could make out what looked like a long wooden wall, with a tower constructed at either end.

As they thumped into the jetty, Julius spotted the unmistakeable figures of Roman legionaries standing atop the towers and along the wall, keeping watch over the comings and goings of the small port.

"That must be a fort," said Cornelius. "The Romans must have a lot of troublemakers keeping them busy."

"Look at him all dressed up in his warm furs!" blurted Julius.

"It gets a BIT NIPPY up here," called out Septimus as he breezed past the trembling animals. "You might want to get yourselves wrapped up!"

"You know, Milus," sighed Julius, "I'm so glad your cheery, furry little face is always around to fill me with the joys of spring."

"COME ON, CHOP, CHOP! Don't just stand there!" barked Septimus. "Get your packs and follow me."

They grabbed their belongings from the hold and were led up the jetty to a waiting horse-drawn cart.

"Jump on the back. We're heading straight to Londinium and we need to get there before dark. SO NO MESSING AROUND!"

Septimus marched off to fix the reins of the horses and Julius looked over to the beach. "Say what you want about Britannia, but that really *is* a lovely beach."

"Just look at all those rock pools," said Rufus. "I bet you could find some crabs in there."

"Ooh!" cried Felix. "I bet there are some BRILLIANT rocks, too!" He dashed over to the water's edge and rifled through the pebbles and stones that lay scattered about in the mud.

Meanwhile, Lucia and Rufus were paddling in a big rock pool with a fishing net trying to find something to catch.

"THERE!" cried Rufus. "A little crab! Get the little nipper! Get him!"

Cornelius joined Julius on the beach wearing his sun hat.

"Nice hat, Cornelius," said Julius.

"Why, thank you," said Cornelius, giving it a slight adjustment. "I know it's cold, but this hat makes me feel like I'm on holiday."

Suddenly, Septimus appeared, looming over them. "HAVE YOU ALL GONE INSANE?!" he screamed, pulling at his hair.

"NOW GET YOUR HAIRY BOTTOMS ON THAT CART!!! IMMEDIATELY!"

Julius, Cornelius, Lucia and Rufus all dashed back to the cart, where they found Milus lounging at the back. He just tutted and shook his head at them in disbelief.

"WAIT!" cried Julius. "Where's Felix?"

From the beach came a strained cry from their friend. "JULIUS! GUYS! COME AND GIVE ME A HAND!!"

"That antelope is going to get us in so much trouble," huffed Julius. "Come on, before Septimus notices."

Back on the beach, Felix was struggling with his bulging knapsack.

They all grabbed the pack between them and tried to lift it up, but it was impossible.

"This is ridiculous!" gasped Julius. "What have you *got* in there?"

"It's my rock collection," said Felix. "I take it everywhere I go."

"We're going to have to drag it," said Cornelius. "And be quick about it, before Septimus sees us and explodes like Mount Vesuvius."

Between them they were able to pull it over to the cart, but they still couldn't lift it onto the back.

"I'm sorry Felix," said Julius. "But you're going to have to lose some of your rocks. You can't carry this pack around everywhere."

"NOOOO!" cried Felix. "You can't make me!" He tried again to heft his pack up, but it was to no avail and he finally collapsed in a heap. A small tear trickled down his cheek.

Cornelius sat next to Felix and put his arm round him. "Come on old chap," he said. "Maybe pick your all-time favourites and we can go from there. I bet there's some you don't really need."

Felix just sat there looking glum. "But I love ALL my rocks…"

"We can help you choose!" said Lucia. She convinced Felix to empty his knapsack and lay out all his rocks neatly on the ground. Everyone stood back in awe at the strange and wonderful collection.

"To be fair," said Julius, "that *is* a pretty amazing collection!"

What in the name of JUPITER is going on here?

"We're trying to help Felix with his rock collection," said Julius. "He's having trouble deciding which ones to keep and which ones to leave behind."

Septimus grabbed a handful of the rocks, walked over to the water's edge and hurled them into the sea.

"There. Easy," he said, brushing his hands. "Now let's MOVE IT!"

CHAPTER NINE
LONDINIUM CALLING

Julius boggled at the endless green fields and ancient woodland as their cart rolled along the smooth Roman road. Occasionally, in the distance dotted here and there, he could spot odd-looking round houses with roofs of straw and walls of mud. "Why did the Romans come to Britannia? It's just fields and trees!" said Julius. "I've not seen one person out here yet."

"Don't worry," replied Rufus, who was keeping a watchful eye. "I'm sure we'll come across some of those gangly weirdos before you know it!"

Bored with looking at fields, Julius snuggled down among the packs and drifted off to sleep.

In his dreams he found himself being chased by a tall, scary monkey.

"LEAVE ME ALONE!" cried Julius, as he tried to escape through a muddy field, but the monkey was fast and soon caught up with him. As Julius turned to face the monkey, he noticed that it was wearing a pair of stripy trousers. "'ERE!" cried Julius. "Are you wearing my LEGS?"

"No!" came a familiar voice. "He's wearing *MY* LEGS!"

"Oh, BROTHER!" cried Julius. "Have you come to set me FREE?"

BRUTUS??

"DON'T LET THEM STEAL YOUR LEGS, JULIUS!" said Brutus.

"I WON'T!" sobbed Julius. "I WON'T LET THEM STEAL MY LEGS!"

No one's stealing your legs! Get off me you idiot!

"WAKE UP YOU LAZY LOT!" roared Septimus. "WE'RE HERE!"

Through the murk of the dusk, Julius could make out the unmistakeable shapes of Roman buildings, standing square and tall along the bank.

"Welcome to **LONDINIUM!**" said Septimus.

As Julius rubbed his tired eyes, he was greeted by a noisy, bustling port. His nostrils were hit by the very familiar pong of a city, as the cart rumbled over a long wooden bridge which crossed the great snaking river.

"Cor!" he said, taking in the view. "This must be where everybody was hiding. Check out all of those ships!"

"Merchant ships," said Cornelius. "The Romans need their home comforts. You can bet those boats are filled with wine and olive oil and all that stinky fish sauce they slap on everything that moves."

"It looks like they're taking lots of stuff away too," said Julius. "Look at all those poor sheep and cows being piled onto that ship. I don't envy their journey."

"NOW you know why the Romans are here," said Cornelius. "They need to feed and clothe that growing Empire of theirs."

"Keep an eye out for those vicious BRITONS, though," warned Julius, ducking down in the cart. "They're not getting MY stripy legs!"

"I think you'll find they're everywhere!" smiled Cornelius.

"Yeah!" said Rufus. "And you know what? They look pretty ordinary to me!"

Julius peeked out from in between the packs and stared at all the strange-looking people going about their business.

I suppose they do...

"But it's COLD!" protested Julius. "Why aren't they trying to kill us for our furs?"

"I think maybe Cornelius has been listening to too many scared Romans!" laughed Rufus.

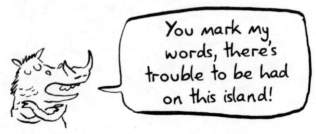

You mark my words, there's trouble to be had on this island!

"Rufus is probably right," said Julius. "We don't have a thing to worry about. This place looks as normal as anywhere! The tournament is going to be a BREEZE. Like Hadrian said, the locals will LOVE us."

After trundling through the city, the cart suddenly took a sharp left, revealing a wooden amphitheatre up ahead. "OOH! I think we've found our holiday home!" squealed Julius.

CHAPTER TEN
HOME FROM HOME

"It's a lot smaller than I expected," said Julius, looking the amphitheatre up and down. "That gives me hope – their home crowd won't be anywhere near as noisy as the Colosseum's. We'll *easily* win in there!"

The small amphitheatre was surrounded by fields, but just behind it sat an imposing stone fort.

"COR!" gasped Cornelius. "That fort must be home to A THOUSAND soldiers. Look at the size of it!"

Septimus laughed as he pulled the cart up next to a ramshackle old barn. "You must be JOKING if you think we're going to let a bunch of STINKING FLEABAGS LIKE YOU stay in our fort."

He grabbed their knapsacks off the cart and chucked them onto the ground.

"THIS is where YOU LOT are staying during your little 'holiday'!" he grinned.

Julius jumped off the cart, grumbling. "You can't expect us to stay in there, it's FREEZING!"

Septimus rubbed his hands together to keep warm as a biting wind blew through the city. "You'd best

huddle up close together to keep warm tonight."
He chuckled. "I don't want any of you dying of
hypothermia, Hadrian would be VERY displeased!"

Septimus climbed back onto the cart. "Our
tournament starts in two days, so we'll have a nice
long training session tomorrow to get you warmed
up. SEE YOU AT THE CRACK OF DAWN!" With
that, he merrily trundled off towards the fort.

The sky suddenly darkened and with a crack of
thunder, a great downpour of rain fell on the city.

"Quick! Get inside the barn!" said Lucia.

They crashed through the rotten door to find a foul, damp hovel, strewn with mouldy straw and bales of stinking hay. Rain streamed in through holes in the roof.

Milus stood up and brushed wet straw from his fur. "Well, this is just BRILLIANT!" he growled. "When these sneaky Romans finally chuck my broken body into some cold, wet ditch somewhere, can you please make sure it says 'I TOLD YOU SO!' on my tombstone."

Milus hurled his knapsack to the floor, but, as the bag landed, a huge squeak screamed out. Everybody turned and looked at the pack.

"I know that squeak..." whispered Cornelius.

"Thanks for leaving me behind, AGAIN!" he screeched. "I teach you ALL my fighting techniques, I turn you into SUPERSTARS, and what thanks do I get? NONE!" He sat down and started nibbling on a biscuit.

"Have you been in Milus's pack all this time?" said Julius.

"What of it?" replied Pliny, spitting crumbs everywhere. "I wasn't going to show my face and get roped into scrubbing ship's decks. Do you think I'm STUPID or something?"

"So, what's the score, anyway?" asked Pliny. "I heard you lot talking about going on 'holibobs'. Where are we then? It's not warm, so it can't be Egypt."

"Britannia!" said Julius.

Pliny nearly choked on his biscuit.

"Then you've HAD it!" he cried. "This island is the LAST place you want to be!"

"But Hadrian says we're going to inspire the locals," said Julius. "He's set up a tournament for us and EVERYTHING! We're the People's Champions!"

"The People's Nincompoops, more like," said Pliny. "The locals don't need entertaining, they need OVERPOWERING!"

"What do you mean?" gasped Julius.

"The Britons are on the verge of REVOLT!" said Pliny. "I heard all about it in the Colosseum. I get ALL my gossip there. The Senate are proper scared about the WHOLE situation. Hadrian is obviously using your so-called popularity as a show of his strength to shut up these whining Britons AND the Senators."

"But if you lot fail to impress these barbarians and they carry on being a bunch of troublemakers, the Senate will FORCE Hadrian to start a very expensive war against Britannia."

"But we're training tomorrow," whimpered Julius. "Then our first fight is the day after. We don't have much time!"

CHAPTER ELEVEN
MUD, SWEAT AND TEARS

The next morning, big blobs of water dripped off Julius's nose as icy rain spat down outside the wooden amphitheatre. Septimus marched up and down, wrapped up warm and dry in his nice thick furs, as he inspected the line of animals.

Right you 'orrible lot!

Get down and give me fifty press-ups!

"WHAT?!" spluttered Julius. "Press-ups in this cold wet mud? You must be joking!"

Septimus leaned close up to Julius's face. "DO I LOOK LIKE I'M JOKING?"

"Now that you mention it, no, you don't..." stammered Julius.

"Good," declared Septimus. "YOU can give me a hundred!"

Julius refused to get on the ground. "This is SO unfair, Septimus. You can't make us train in this horrible cold!"

"Yeah!" said Felix. "It's all right for *you* wrapped up all nice and warm."

"Right!" said Septimus. "Then let me introduce you to an old Roman army trick for warming up." He wandered over to a patch of weeds and grabbed a big handful of nettles.

"I'm not sure I like the look of this..." whispered Julius nervously.

Septimus held up the nettles. "When I was in the 10th Legion fighting barbarians in the FORESTS OF GERMANIA, we didn't SNIVEL about the COLD and WET!"

"What's he going to do?" whispered a perplexed Felix. "Eat them?"

"NO!" continued Septimus. "We thought on our feet. We created SOLUTIONS!" He suddenly whacked Felix's legs with the nettles.

Felix hopped about rubbing his legs, crying in pain. "That REALLY STUNG!" he wailed.

"But are your legs not now warm?" laughed Septimus.

Felix stopped leaping about and had a good look at his red, throbbing legs.

"We're warm! We're warm!" shrieked Cornelius as they all sprinted off across the field.

"Well," said Septimus. "Seeing as you're all running about, I want you to jog around the fort, up to the river, then back here again."

"EXACTLY!" barked Septimus. "CHOP! CHOP! Get moving you 'orrible donkey!"

The animals ran off towards the fort behind the amphitheatre, huffing and puffing as they went.

"I hate running!" spluttered Felix. "I've got flat hooves."

"I'm still exhausted after our training with Pliny last night. I can barely feel my claws!" moaned Lucia.

Julius suddenly sprinted past them all.

Everyone ran up to the strange hut with its pointy straw roof and tiny door.

"Do you think anyone is inside?" asked Julius.

"I saw smoke coming out of the top of the roof, so there must be," said Lucia.

"But what if it's those horrible warriors from the woods?" asked Felix.

"They were in completely the opposite direction," said Rufus.

"Oh yeah," replied Felix and he nudged the door open.

As he poked his head in, Felix suddenly let out a MASSIVE SCREAM, causing everyone else to scream as well. They all ran away from the hovel as fast their legs could carry them.

"COME BACK!" yelled Julius to Felix. "WHY ARE WE RUNNING AWAY?"

"I SAW SOMETHING MOVE!" Felix screeched.

Suddenly, he smacked right into a big wet lump standing in the middle of the field.

"SEPTIMUS!"

"Quite correct, imbecile!" growled Septimus, rain dripping down his red, angry face. "And you're going to regret EVER running away!"

❦CHAPTER TWELVE❦
BRITONS GOT TALENT

The next morning, the animals got up at sunrise and dashed to the wooden arena, where Septimus was already waiting for them.

"EVERYBODY ON THE FLOOR AND GIVE ME ONE HUNDRED PRESS UPS!"

As they sprang into action, Septimus marched up and down very sternly.

"Now you listen to me, you 'ORRIBLE LOT!"

Everyone looked up, but no one dared stop their exercises.

"Today is the first day of our glorious TOURNAMENT! Hadrian has chosen you lot, FOOLISHLY, to my mind, to REPRESENT ROME against the BRITONS!"

Lucia put up her claw. Septimus spun round and glared at the crocodile. "This had better be GOOD!" he whistled through his gritted teeth.

Septimus's eyes nearly popped out with rage. He thrust his stick in her belly. "You. Give me one hundred star jumps! NOW!"

Septimus continued with his speech. "You'll be up against Britannia's GREATEST animal gladiators and I'm expecting YOU to prove Rome's MIGHT and send them packing, thus soothing the BRITONS' angry little brains and eradicating any thoughts they might have about rising up against their wonderful Roman benefactors. UNDERSTAND?"

Benefactors!? Don't you mean "Evil Conquerors"?

Septimus picked Felix up by the scruff of his neck. "You do realise that GERMANIA is a lot further from here than it was from Rome? I'm going to have to kick you EVEN HARDER up the backside to get you there if you don't shut up WITH YOUR BABBLING!"

"So sorry, Septimus," whimpered Felix. "Would you like me to give you another hundred press-ups?"

Septimus dropped Felix back on the ground. "That would be very kind of you, thank you."

"Now this tournament begins in TWO HOURS," roared Septimus, "so I want you dressed and ready for combat in ONE! Do NOT be late!" And he stalked off back to the Roman fort.

The animals flopped to the floor, exhausted. But before they had a chance to catch their breath, Pliny the mouse scuttled into view.

"Oh, look out!" said Julius.

"YES, 'LOOK OUT', INDEED!" snapped the tiny mouse.

"What was THAT for?" shouted Julius.

"'WHAT WAS THAT FOR'? You abandoned me in Rome, then you abandon me in this crazy place. What's *wrong* with me? Do I smell of *cheese* or something?"

"A little," said Julius, rubbing his shin.

Cornelius kicked Julius on his other leg. "Shush!" he said.

"We don't know what we're up against here," squeaked Pliny, "so let's make sure we're ready for ANYTHING!"

❦CHAPTER THIRTEEN❧
PIGS MIGHT FLY

With the tournament minutes away from starting, the arena was already packed with a mix of Roman dignitaries and rowdy Britons.

Julius and Cornelius peeked through the gateway to check out the audience.

Cornelius looked towards the north entrance of the arena where their enemies would appear from. "I wonder who we're up against? I must say, I really don't fancy my chances against a bear."

See any half-naked savages?

Not yet...

A big hand slapped onto Cornelius's shoulder.

"FEAR NOT, WARTHOG!" barked Septimus. "We have a special adversary for you, 'piggy'!"

The cornicen suddenly parped their horns to declare that the games had begun.

"Good luck, Cornelius!" said Julius. "Show those Brits who's boss!"

"Yeah! Kick some Briton BUTT!" yelled Pliny.

In the arena, the Summa Rudis marched into the centre and raised his arms to silence the crowd.

"CITIZENS OF THE ROMAN EMPIRE!" he

cried. A wave of angry BOOs rippled around the arena. The Summa Rudis let out a nervous cough. "Welcome to BRITONS GOT TALENT, where we pit ROMAN versus BRITON, as we bring you CHAMPIONS from the city of Rome itself!"

"In our first fight today," continued the Summa Rudis, "we will witness PIG VERSUS PIG!"

"WHAT?!" cried Cornelius. "I ... I don't understand..."

A bloodthirsty cheer erupted around the tiny stadium.

"What sort of pigs do they have out here, then?" asked Julius.

"Err, THAT sort!" said Felix, pointing to the other end of the arena.

"FLIPPIN' 'ECK. He's like a shaved version of Cornelius!" said Rufus.

"From Britannia," continued the Summa Rudis, "we have PERICLES THE PIG!" A great roar went up, shaking the wooden structure of the stadium. "And from Rome, CORNELIUS THE WARTHOG!"

Cornelius stumbled out to the centre of the arena to a mix of cheers and boos.

Pericles the pig looked unimpressed. "Not *him*!" he growled. "I want the zebra!"

The Summa Rudis tried to placate him. "I'm afraid you don't understand, Pericles. There isn't a *choice* of opponent, you have to fight the warthog."

"No, Roman, YOU don't understand!"

The crowd rose to their feet as Pericles confronted poor Cornelius, "And that means YOU TOO, ROMAN HOG!"

The enraged Pericles stood bellowing and snorting at the Roman arena gate. "THE ZEBRA!" he roared. "BRING ME THE ZEBRA! I WILL BRING YOU ROMANS DOWN!"

"Well, that's a good start," gulped Julius.

The agitated crowd started booing and chanting,
"ROMANS OUT! ROMANS OUT!"

Septimus signalled to two watching soldiers to drag Pericles away.

"No, donkey, it is NOT a good start," growled Septimus.

"Maybe I should go on next, to calm the crowd," said Julius. "Who's the next opponent?"

"Douglas the sheep," replied Septimus.

"A SHEEP?" laughed Felix. "Sheep are stupid bumbling creatures!"

SKIP!

Leave this to ME!

"WAIT!" cried Septimus. "THIS IS NO ORDINARY SHEEP…" But it was too late. Felix skipped into the arena, greeted by boos and laughter.

The blast of the cornicen horns and the roar of the crowd signalled the entrance of Felix's opponent.

"AAIIEE! *YOU'RE* NOT A SHEEP!" screamed
Felix. "YOU'RE *A MONSTER!*"

"ARE YOUSE THE ZEBRA?" growled Douglas, thumping his shield against his horns like a drum.

"Um … no," whimpered Felix. "I'm the antelope."

"Then YOUSE GOING DOWN, ROMAN!"

The crowd roared their approval.

Back at the gate Julius put his head in his hooves.

"This really isn't going to end well."

The cornicen marked the start of the fight and the grizzled sheep didn't waste any time in battering his sword against Felix's shield.

Much to everyone's surprise, the plucky antelope held his ground against the relentless blows.

But suddenly the sheep jogged away to the far side of the arena. Julius turned to Pliny and the others and shrugged his shoulders. "Where's he going?"

"Maybe these Britons aren't as tough as we thought," laughed Pliny. "Felix has got him on the run!"

"I wouldn't bet on it," warned Milus.

Douglas the sheep bent forward, pointing his unwieldy horns in Felix's direction, and bellowed, "YOUSE ROMANS CAN'T PUSH US AROUND ANY MORE!! YOUSE ARE GOING DOWN!"

The crowd stood up and cheered their approval.

A furious and desperate Septimus turned to Julius. "GET OUT THERE, DONKEY!" he screamed. "Fight for the pride of Rome! And if you DON'T win, YOU AND YOUR PATHETIC FRIENDS WILL *NEVER* SEE FREEDOM AGAIN!"

☙ CHAPTER FOURTEEN ☙
HOO NOO BROON COO!

Septimus shoved Julius out into the arena. "NOW MAKE YOUR EMPEROR PROUD!" he bellowed.

A great roar erupted from the crowd as Julius strutted to the centre of the arena.

In Rome only a few weeks ago, Julius had entered the Colosseum the people's hero, but out here it was a different story entirely; out here the audience saw Julius as the enemy and hated him and all his fellow Roman gladiators.

He'd already seen Cornelius and Felix soundly thrashed by the ferocious Britons. He was going to have to draw on all his training and experience to get him through the next few minutes.

Back at the gate, Lucia, Rufus, Milus and Pliny looked on anxiously.

"This crowd REALLY hates us," said Rufus.

"Actually, they hate the Romans and that includes US!" replied Lucia, biting her claws.

"I'm not sure I'm that keen on being called a Roman," whispered Rufus, trying not to let Septimus hear him.

"Me neither," said Lucia.

"We'll let Julius fight this next gladiator, then we'll make a run for it," whispered Rufus.

"Good idea," said Lucia. "I'll start thinking of an escape plan. You in, Milus?"

The familiar PARP of the cornicen trumpets finally heralded the entrance of Julius's opponent.

"ALL THE WAY FROM THE HIGHLANDS OF CALEDONIA," cried the Summa Rudis, "BERTA THE COW!"

From the opposite gate stomped in the biggest, hairiest cow Julius, or any of the others, had ever seen.

"COR!" cried Pliny. "Look at the horns on THAT!"

As the
Summa Rudis
drew the two
adversaries
together, Julius
gasped at the
size of his
opponent.

"Are YOUSE supposed to be THE MIGHTY
ZEEBRA?" rasped Berta, poking Julius in the stomach.
"Ye no look so mighty from where AH'M standing!"

The trumpets
signalled the start
of the fight and
Julius immediately
shoved the huge
cow with his shield,
forcing her to
stumble backwards.
The audience let
out a gasp.

The embarrassed Berta held up her massive two-handed sword above her head and rushed at Julius with a great ROAR, bringing the blade thumping down onto Julius's shield, sending thundering shockwaves through his body.

"Coo! I felt THAT!" shuddered Pliny.

"I think the whole amphitheatre did," said Lucia, peeking through her claws.

Berta didn't let up and unleashed a volley of blows against the valiant but ultimately over-powered zebra, pinning him to the floor.

"Haven't youse got it into yer head yet, zeebra?" spat Berta. "We NO WANT youse Romans here!"

"I don't think I want to be here EITHER!" cried Julius.

The crowd were going wild. Some of them even started ripping up the wooden stadium seats and chucking the broken slats into the arena.

Septimus had seen enough.

Gathering all his strength, Julius let out a great yell. He charged at the enormous cow with his shield and flew into an attack with his sword, but Berta easily parried him away, sending Julius crashing to the floor.

He leapt up, but with a swipe of the handle of her sword, Berta sent Julius flying, knocking his helmet right off his head.

The cow raised her massive sword for one final blow.

The dazed Julius braced himself behind his shield, his energy and resolve finally spent.

"JULIUS! NOOOOO!" cried a desperate Lucia.

CLXXXIII

The whole arena exploded with a deep roar from the crowd. The Empire's so-called great zebra champion and ALL the Roman gladiators were BEATEN!

Some of the audience began climbing over the arena wall and chanting abuse at the Roman dignitaries. Big chunks of wooden seating rained down, sending the Romans running for their lives.

The unruly crowd then turned on the handful of cowering Roman soldiers who were struggling to keep the situation under control.

"GET THAT STRIPY IDIOT BACK HERE AT ONCE!" Septimus screamed.

Rufus and Lucia sprinted to their stricken friend, who lay semi-conscious on the arena floor, the rampaging crowd threatening to trample him underfoot.

Let's get him out of here quickly!

Septimus shepherded them all out of the back gate and straight into the Roman fort next door, as the amphitheatre erupted into chaos.

As the giant gates of the fort slammed shut behind them, Septimus exploded into a frenzy.

"HADRIAN WILL BE HEARING ABOUT THIS OUTRAGE!" he yelled. "IN FACT, I'VE A GOOD MIND TO SEND YOU ALL PACKING BACK TO ROME!"

He grabbed Julius and pulled him right up to his face.

"You have another fight in two days, donkey. Prepare to be trained to within an inch of YOUR MISERABLE, FURRY LIFE!"

CHAPTER FIFTEEN
HOLE LOT OF TROUBLE

The next morning Septimus put Julius and his friends through their most punishing training regime EVER.

Felix was really starting to struggle. "THESE PRESS-UPS ARE KILLING ME!" he cried. "I CAN'T FEEL MY ARMS!!"

Septimus stormed over. "What's that, goat? You can't feel your arms, you say?"

"No..." whimpered the floundering antelope.

"Then let's work on those RIDICULOUS SPINDLY LEGS OF YOURS!"

Soon they all collapsed with exhaustion, dizzy and discombobulated from all their exercise.

"GOOD WORK!" barked Septimus. "Have a little rest, because we're off for a twenty mile cross-country run in five minutes."

"We don't stand a chance against those Briton beasts no matter HOW much we train!" whimpered Felix. "I don't know what they eat out here, but they're MONSTERS!"

Lucia sidled up to Julius. "Fear not," she whispered. "I have formulated an escape plan!" And she tapped the side of her nose.

"But how?" said Julius. "Septimus will be watching us like a hawk after last time."

"Don't worry," she said, tapping her nose again. "Just watch me."

"No dressing up?"

"No dressing up!" the crocodile promised.

Septimus looked at Lucia suspiciously. "WAITAMINUTE!" he said. "You must think I'm STUPID!"

"What ever do you mean?" replied Lucia innocently.

"If you think I'm going to let you go running on your own after LAST TIME, you've got another thing coming. I'm going with you!"

"Of course!" said Lucia, and they all ran off towards the fort.

As they reached the fort, Lucia jogged up next to Septimus.

"So, have you had much of a chance to look around Britannia since we arrived, Septimus?" she asked politely.

"WHAT?" replied Septimus gruffly. "No I haven't, not while I've had to keep an eye on YOU ODDBALLS!"

"Oh, it really *is* a lovely place," she said. "Rolling hills and beautiful meadows to rival even Rome itself."

"In fact, the wet seasons here create a *gorgeous* lush green landscape."

"SHOW ME these meadows, crocodile,"
said Septimus. "I am rather partial to collecting
wildflowers. They can often be useful ingredients for
the infusion of balms and oils."

Lucia winked at the others.

"He does like his bathing oils, old Septimus,"
whispered Julius.

As they trotted across the fields and around
marshlands, Lucia dutifully pointed out interesting
plants and natural wonders.

They skirted round the edge of the ancient woodlands, keeping a beady eye out for any shifty-looking warriors who might jump out with their bows and arrows.

Finally, they reached the boggy puddles that Rufus had cleverly steered the gang through whilst escaping the local barbarians.

"Yes, good plan!" agreed Septimus, admiring the view. "And when we get back, we can finish off with FIFTY STAR JUMPS!"

"But Septimus, we can jump *here*!" cried Lucia.

"Yes, that looks like BRILLIANT fun!" said Felix, and he and Rufus both joined in, leaping from puddle to puddle.

"Come on Julius and Cornelius!" called out Lucia with a cheeky wink. "And you Milus. You could definitely do with some cheering up!"

"YOUR TURN!" shouted Lucia to Septimus.

Septimus huffed with indignation. "You are, of course, joking."

"Oh come on, Septimus!" cried Felix. "Jump away all that tension! No one's looking!"

Septimus grimaced, his eyes swivelling from one side to the other, to see if anyone might actually be watching. He took a deep breath and snorted through his big hairy nostrils.

"Oh, GO ON THEN!" he muttered.

"SEE?" shouted Lucia. "Isn't it FUN?!"

As Septimus gleefully hopped from one big puddle to the next, Lucia suddenly pointed to a MASSIVE puddle just up ahead. "Check out the size of THAT one!" she squealed. "YOU have it, Septimus."

"OF *COURSE* I SHOULD HAVE IT!" he bellowed. And he took an enormous run up, before leaping into the air like a graceful gazelle.

"I KNOW!" cried Lucia. "That's the puddle Rufus fell into up to his neck! I saved it especially for Septimus!"

"QUICKLY!" shouted Julius. "Let's leg it before he surfaces!" And they ran away as fast as they could.

As they leapt over hedges and across fields, Cornelius suddenly slapped his face.

"PLINY!" he cried. "We forgot PLINY again!"

"No we didn't," said Milus, and he opened a pouch attached to his belt.

"Lucia warned me of her plan and I thought we should probably bring the little scallywag along for the ride," said Milus.

"What?" said Julius, confused. "You *knew* about the puddle plan beforehand?"

"You think I'd be merrily jumping in puddles otherwise?" Milus snarled.

"Hmm ... I *did* wonder!" said Felix.

"And do you have a plan as to what we do NOW, Lucia?" squeaked Cornelius. "We're in the middle of nowhere!"

"Follow me!" she said, before jogging off.

As they followed her over a hill, Lucia pointed to a familiar-looking round hut, with smoke drifting out of its tall, pointed roof.

"We're staying here tonight!" smiled the crocodile. "They'll never think of looking for us here." Lucia ran up to the small door and gave it a gentle knock.

"But there's a GHOST living in there!" screamed Felix, backing away slowly. "I saw it with my own eyeballs!"

"You saw no such thing," said Milus.

"But what if it's the home of MAD BARBARIAN WARRIORS?" asked a worried Julius.

"Then we just look for somewhere else to stay," replied Lucia, shrugging her shoulders. "Simple!"

Suddenly, the little wooden door creaked open and a strange, pungent smell wafted out of the hut.

A hooded old lady shuffled into the doorway. "Do come in," she smiled. "I've just been cooking a broth…"

CHAPTER SIXTEEN
BOIL AND BUBBLE

"Why are we here?" whispered Julius, looking around the eerie hovel. "This place gives me the CREEPS!"

"You are free to leave," croaked the old lady. "Do you think me glad to have the likes of a lion and a crocodile prowling about my house?"

"Y-yeah, she's right," gulped Felix, "we should go and find somewhere else to sleep, I'll see you guys later..."

"You're going nowhere," said Rufus, pulling Felix back by the horns.

"Please excuse my friends," apologised Lucia.
"We're just looking for somewhere to stay the night."

Um, we're gladiators from Rome...

"I *know* who you are!" said the old crone, turning towards the warthog and staring deep into his eyes. "You are *Romans*, but I believe there is more to you than meets the eye."

She shuffled to the middle of the room where a large iron cauldron bubbled away, the source of the overpowering stench. "I have been making *a broth*, you are most welcome to partake with me..."

SLURP!

She immediately coughed and retched, spitting it back into the cauldron. "Needs more salt," she said, and shuffled to one of her shelves to pick up a small bowl of salt crystals.

Felix pulled a face of disgust at Julius, sticking out his tongue. "I ain't eating it," he whispered. "You can't *make* me!"

Lucia gave the antelope a swift kick in the shin to shut him up.

"I heard word of your contest yesterday. *There is much trouble in the air*," croaked the old lady as she handed out bowls of broth.

The Romans are weak ... and the people know it.

"We were brought over here to demonstrate how strong Rome is," said Julius helpfully.

"A last throw of the dice from a weak emperor!" rasped the old lady. "War is coming and he knows it, we all know it. And there's nothing Hadrian can do to stop it."

"That's what I'VE been trying to tell 'em!" piped up Pliny, poking his head out of Milus's pouch. "These Romans are SCOUNDRELS, I wouldn't trust them as far as I could THROW them!"

The old lady laughed at the feisty mouse.

"Would you like some broth too, *little warrior*? I have plenty to go around."

"Will you now," growled Milus.

"Excuse me, but if the Romans are so weak," said Julius as he supped his broth, "then what do any of you have to fear?"

The old crone stared into the hearth. "Because our own leaders *are weak*! We have plenty of fighting men, but they are a rabble that lack leadership."

"Boudicca?" said Julius. "Who's Boudicca?"

Ahem! Boudicca is the Warrior Queen who nearly defeated the Romans sixty years ago!

"Your hairy friend knows his history well!" laughed the old lady. "I was at the Warrior Queen's side when we nearly drove these Roman cockroaches away all those years ago."

"COR! How exciting!" exclaimed Lucia.

The crone continued. "So *fearsome* was our Queen, that she almost rid every nook and cranny of our land of these vermin. The mad Emperor Nero himself was ready to order his army's retreat and leave us as they had found us." She let out a deep sigh and shook her head. *"But t'was not to be…"*

The crone stood up to collect the empty bowls. "If Boudicca could see how our chieftains crawl and bow to the Roman invaders today," she rasped, "she would *rip out her own heart!*"

"Seems a bit drastic," whispered Felix to Julius.

"Please, tell us more about Boudicca," urged Lucia. "She sounds FIERCE!"

"Oh, my dear, Boudicca was a warrior *so brave and ingenious*, why, when she flew into battle on her chariot…"

"SHE RODE A CHARIOT?" gasped Lucia. "By the gods, I love her ALREADY!!"

Lucia nearly fainted. "Oh, but I couldn't, it's too precious."

The old crone shuffled over to the cloak and unhooked it. "Put it on, child. Our Queen would share her mantle with one so courageous."

Lucia held the soft woollen cloak out in front of her. The orange and red checks looked as fresh as the day it was made. She swept it behind her and tied two corners round her neck.

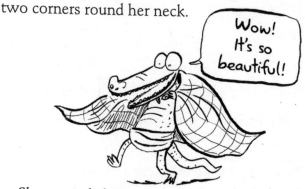

She started skipping around the room. "I want to be a Queen riding into battle on my chariot!"

The old lady chuckled. "Oh, *how* we Britons need another Boudicca today!"

"'ERE! I want to dress up too!" said Julius. "But I want some of those blue drawings that our opponents had!"

The old lady tottered to one of her shelves. "Then I have just the thing for you!"

She showed Julius a pot of blue paste. "This is *woad*. It is what our warriors use to paint patterns onto their bodies. *Would you like to try some?*"

"You must choose an animal whose image would provoke FEAR in your enemies!" said the old lady.

Felix piped up. "Have a SPIDER, Julius. I hate spiders!"

"Good answer. A spider it is then!" said Julius.

The crone cackled, then dipped her finger in the paste and started drawing on Julius's chest.

After ten minutes, she sat back and admired her handiwork. "Well, what do you think?"

"Then why *don't* you?" said the old lady.

"What do you mean?" said Julius.

"*TAKE ON THE WORLD!*" She clapped. "Bearing the drawings of these creatures gives you their POWER! You can be *UNBEATABLE*!"

She gathered the animals around her and whispered to them. "You'll find that Pericles, Douglas and Berta are really no different from you; they're slaves just as much as you are. Go back and show Londinium who you REALLY are."

Be the CHAMPIONS that everyone says you are!

"You might find that you'll make more friends than enemies AND rid us of the Roman scourge *once and for all*!"

CHAPTER SEVENTEEN
WHEN IN LONDINIUM

The next day, with the words of the old lady ringing in their ears, Julius and his friends headed back to Londinium and the awaiting crowds of the amphitheatre. This time they were determined to carry out what Hadrian and Septimus had demanded of them – to win over the Briton crowd. But this time it would be on their OWN terms.

I KNEW you'd come crawling back.

"I ought to have you ARRESTED for leaving me in that big puddle yesterday," growled Septimus.

"MAKE WAY," said Julius, as he pushed past the Lanista. "We're here to do our job!"

As the animals strode to the arena, Septimus did a double take at their tattoo-covered bodies.

The cornicen horns triumphantly blared, heralding the arrival of the Roman champions.

Julius and his tattooed friends burst defiantly out into the arena to a great ROAR of approval from the crowd.

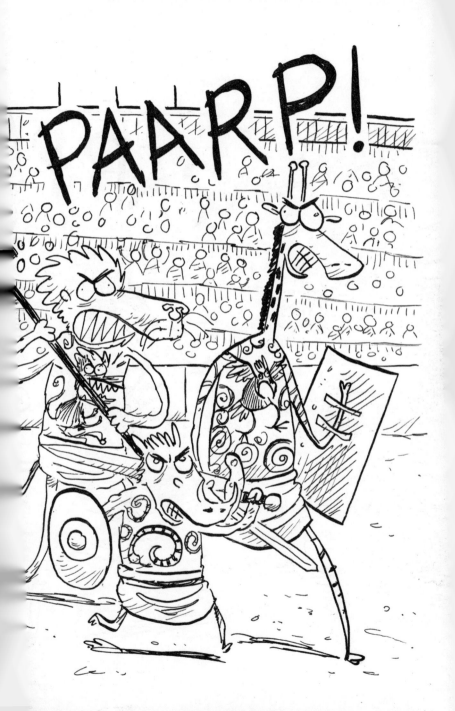

Pericles, Douglas and Berta looked on astonished.

In the centre of the arena, the Summa Rudis
gathered all the gladiators together.

"WHO IS TO FIGHT FIRST?"

"I'll go first," growled Milus.

"Then so shall I," rasped Douglas the sheep.

The other gladiators dispersed to their gates and the
two animals sized each other up. Douglas prodded the

drawing on Milus's chest with his sword. "And what's that WEE BEASTIE meant to be, then?"

The cornicens blared and the crowd cheered as the fight began.

The brutish sheep wasted no time in thrusting his sword towards Milus, but the nimble lion easily dodged out of the way of the deadly blade.

"Ye know, Romans wearing woad tattoos is a GREAT INSULT to my people!" spat Douglas.

"We're no different from you!" roared Milus.
"We're SLAVES of the Roman Empire, too!"

"'No different'?" laughed Douglas as he lunged with
his sword. "What are ye even TALKING about?"

Milus pole-vaulted on his trident, kicking the
confused sheep's shield out of his hoof.

"We want to HELP you!" said Milus. He thrust his
trident into Douglas's sword and wrenched it away
from the sheep.

"Ye've got a funny way of showing it!" wheezed Douglas, as Milus stood on him, triumphant.

The crowd leapt to their feet. Their own champion may have been beaten, but he was beaten by another renegade of the Empire!

Pericles the pig flew into a rage. "I'M NOT PUTTING UP WITH THIS NONSENSE!" And he raced to the centre of the arena.

"I'd better go out there and face him," said Julius, marching out to great cheers and whistles from the crowd.

In the wings, Septimus was FURIOUS. "WHAT ARE YOU IMBECILES UP TO?! YOU'RE SUPPOSED TO SHUT THE CROWD UP, NOT MAKE THEM *WORSE!*"

The Summa Rudis signalled for the fight to begin and Pericles hammered down axe blows onto Julius's shield. "We're not falling for your TRICKERY, zebra!" he cried out. "We are NOT to be fooled in Britannia. We know you Romans too well!"

"LIES!" cried the pig.

Julius leapt into the air like the spider tattooed on his chest and clonked Pericles on the back of his head.

"JOIN US!" he said to Pericles. "We can take down this Roman army TOGETHER!"

"Why should we join up with WEAKLINGS? We can take on the Roman army without you!"

Pericles didn't have an answer. Julius saw that the pig was momentarily troubled by his taunt and attacked him while he was distracted.

"You knew who I was before I even came here!" cried Julius as he bashed against the pig's axes. "You know what I'm capable of. If I can beat the best in Rome, together WE can be rid of the Roman curse from Britannia!"

Julius stood triumphant and raised his sword into the air.

He turned to the red-faced Septimus and gestured to the chanting crowd. "Consider your Britons WON OVER!" he cried.

Suddenly, out of the blue, a barrage of trumpets sounded and a legion of soldiers poured into the arena. A standard bearer followed, leading a golden chariot pulled by two magnificent white horses. Standing triumphantly on the chariot was Emperor Hadrian himself!

"HADRIAN? HERE?" Julius cried. "I don't understand!"

"You disappoint me!" said Hadrian. "My own champion A TRAITOR!"

CHAPTER EIGHTEEN

HE CAME, HE SAW, HE LOCKED HIM UP

"Take him and his friends and throw them into the dungeon!" commanded Hadrian.

"You're not the Emperor out here, Hadrian!" said Julius defiantly as he was dragged away. "These woad-wearing warriors will rise up and defeat you!"

"SILENCE!" snapped Hadrian. "As a SLAVE of Rome, your words are meaningless."

"While you were out here, plotting with your traitorous friends, our new People's Champion has received special intense training from Victorious himself!"

Hadrian laughed at Julius's confused face. "He's far more loyal to the Empire than you'll ever be, zebra. He doesn't bleat ON and ON demanding his freedom, he WANTS to fight for Rome!"

He leaned in close to Julius's face. "You shall meet him when you battle TO THE DEATH with him at my GRAND NEW PROJECT!"

"New project? Have you built yourself another golden toilet?" scoffed Julius.

"ALL WILL QUAKE WHEN THEY BEAR WITNESS TO ROME'S GREATEST CONSTRUCTION YET...!" declared Hadrian.

"Wait, did Hadrian *really* just get excited about a wall?" whispered Felix.

"These Romans are a funny lot," agreed Cornelius.

The animals were taken down into the dungeons of the Roman fort. As the big metal door clanged shut, Julius let out a deep sigh.

"I think Hadrian turning up surprised everyone, even Septimus," said Cornelius.

Suddenly there came a scurrying noise under the door. A little head popped out through the gap.

"Have you come to rescue us?" asked Felix excitedly.

"Er, nope," said Pliny as he squished his whole body under the door. "But I *have* come bearing good news!

"I was having a natter with those weird Briton gladiators and it seems you and Milus have successfully sown the seeds of rebellion in their minds.

"Turns out that old lady was right! Their Big Cheeses are either useless or in the pockets of the Romans, so you're *exactly* the sort of big noise they can get behind!"

"You know, I've always said there was something special about you, Julius. You're going to have to be the one who takes the bull by the horns, yet again!"

"'ERE! I'm not fighting that big cow again, am I?" said Julius.

"No, Berta is right behind you!" replied Pliny.

"So who IS this new champion, then?" asked Cornelius.

"Not a clue!" said Pliny. "Hadrian is keeping his new pet completely under wraps. Which means we have to make sure Julius is in the best shape EVER to thrash this mystery champion, so we can show the Romans WHO'S BOSS!"

❧ CHAPTER NINETEEN ❧
FINAL FRONTIER

The next morning Julius and the rest of the gladiators were shoved into wooden carts and carried off to the wilds of the northern frontier.

Three long days they endured being cramped up in their boxes. The further north they travelled, the colder it got, and the wetter it got.

On the third day, Lucia suddenly cried out in excitement. "Look!" she shouted. "THE WALL! I can see the wall!"

Everyone craned their necks out of their cages to try to catch a glimpse of Hadrian's latest project.

"Well, that IS a big old wall," said Julius.

"So many ROCKS!" yelped Felix.

Their carts trundled over a bridge and headed towards a great fort that sat at the foot of the wall.

They passed through a huge stone gatehouse and into a busy courtyard teeming with soldiers.

"Well, did you see it?" said Hadrian. "What did you think? Isn't my wall MAGNIFICENT!"

Yeah, we're SO pleased you dragged us hundreds of miles to see a stupid WALL.

"All I care about is finding out who this gladiator I'm up against is!" said Julius.

"All in good time, zebra!" replied Hadrian. "One thing you can be sure about is that he is *a fearsome warrior* and your death tomorrow will be swift!"

As Julius and the others were thrown into another dungeon, Pliny sneaked in carrying a pot of blue paint. "RIGHT, we need to get this People's Champion ready for battle!" he squeaked. Pliny dipped his paw into the paste. "What animal do you want?"

CHAPTER TWENTY
HADRIAN'S BRAWL

Julius and the others were taken from their dungeon to the wooden amphitheatre outside the wall. Inside, the thousand seats were easily filled with the Roman soldiers who served the fort.

Hadrian took his seat alongside Septimus in the royal box. Once settled, he signalled to the Summa Rudis to let the game begin.

"Good luck, Julius!" said Cornelius, giving him a big hug. "The gods are watching over you!"

"Yeah! Good luck Julius!" called out Pliny. "Go kick some ..." Suddenly he choked on his words as he saw exactly who it was that Julius was up against. "... ZEBRA BUTT?!"

Julius could barely believe his eyes. "But HOW?!"

Brutus skipped around, flicking his sword in the air. "Word got to me about your jolly exploits in Rome, so I thought I'd come and get a taste of the action myself!"

He sauntered up to Julius and poked his sword into his brother's chin.

"I find that VERY hard to believe!" cried Julius, swatting Brutus's sword away.

"Victorious HIMSELF told me and HE should know, he's fought LOTS of gladiators. Well done on beating

Victorius, by the way, that *is* quite an achievement."
Brutus flicked his sword again, millimetres away from
Julius's face. "But the difference between me and you
is that I'M not a GREAT BIG CRY BABY!"

Brutus let out a great big laugh. "I always KNEW
you were a massive loser!"

In the wings, Julius's friends were in total shock.
They'd heard that his brother Brutus was a bit of a
scallywag, but they'd never realised he was quite so
mean!

"It must be the Romans talking," said Cornelius. "If he's been hanging around with Victorius, no wonder he's gone mad!"

In the arena, the Summa Rudis separated the two zebras. "Calm down, you two, we haven't even started yet! Wait for my signal."

He held up his stick, waited a few seconds, then brought it down: the fight had officially begun.

Julius immediately took up a defensive position. His brother's swagger told him that Brutus would be over-confident and try for an early win.

Brutus predictably went for the kill, slashing and bashing away at Julius's shield, but Julius held his ground.

From behind his shield, as powerful blows rained down on him, Julius tried to reason with his errant brother.

"I'm not YOU, brother!" cried Brutus as he twirled in the air, showing off his new sword skills. "I'VE been promised a huge villa in the hills of Rome when I thrash you!"

Julius pushed out with his shield, causing Brutus to stumble.

"They promised me MY FREEDOM!" he cried. "And look where that got me!"

Brutus paused for a second, taking in what his brother had just said, but he immediately put it out of his mind.

"No, Brutus! They will chew you up and spit you out! Come with us, help win our freedom and the freedom of ALL these barbarian Britons! You know I'm right!"

I'm not listening!

Julius let out a big sigh. "Well, I tried my best," he said.

Brutus hung back, confused. "What do you mean, 'you tried your best'?"

Julius didn't give him time to think. He leapt into a somersault, landed behind his bewildered brother and smacked him across the back of the head, knocking him out cold.

In the royal box, Hadrian was livid with fury. This was NOT the outcome he'd been promised!

Julius was grabbed by Hadrian's guards as the Emperor raged in his box. "SEIZE THE OTHER BEASTS TOO! DON'T LET ANY OF THEM ESCAPE!"

As Julius was being dragged away, one of Hadrian's soldiers approached the royal box. "Caesar, the other animals are nowhere to be seen!"

"NOWHERE?!" cried Hadrian. "That's ridiculous, where were all my guards?"

"Er..." coughed the soldier nervously. "Watching your gladiators, sir."

"WAIT! SOLDIER!" cried the Emperor. "BRING ME MY SNAKES AND A WINE SACK! I will show these BEASTS that I will NOT BE TRIFLED WITH! Bring the zebra with you!"

At the bottom of the fort was a wide, fast-running, twisting river. "You are trouble, zebra," muttered Hadrian, "and there's only one way we Romans deal with troublemakers."

Two soldiers ran up to the Emperor and presented him with a large sack, a wooden box and a pair of big leather gloves.

Hadrian put the gloves on and opened the box.

There you are, my pretties!

Carefully he picked up one of the snakes by the back of its neck, then gestured to one of the soldiers. "Open the bag and make the zebra stand in it!"

"'ERE! What are you up to, YA WEIRDO?" cried Julius.

The two legionaries wrestled poor Julius into the sack, his arms still tied behind his back. Hadrian smiled as he dropped a squirming snake into the sack.

The second snake was less keen on being handled, but Hadrian deftly grabbed it and released it into the sack.

Julius tried to stay calm as the snakes wriggled around his hooves. "The people of Rome WON'T be happy when they discover what you've done with me!" he bluffed. "You have a fight on your hands here, and you'll have one at home too!"

"Oh, get over yourself!" snapped Hadrian. "You're not that important. Champion gladiators come and go like the wind." He gestured to the soldiers. "Sew this windbag up!"

The soldiers pulled the sack over Julius's head and quickly stitched it up.

"NOW THROW HIM IN THE RIVER AND LET'S BE OFF."

CHAPTER TWENTY-ONE
HE AIN'T HEAVY...

Julius tried not to panic. Although, to be fair there was plenty to panic about. He was stuck in an airtight sack with two venomous snakes and they'd just been thrown into the river. He'd been in scrapes before, but this one was ... well, scrapier.

Julius decided that he would try to reason with the snakes. "Now listen guys, we're in a bit of a tight situation here, so let's try to not get too bitey, eh?"

"Er, excuse me," said the other snake. "Are you by any chance JULIUS Zebra?"

"Um ... why yes, I am, actually," replied Julius.

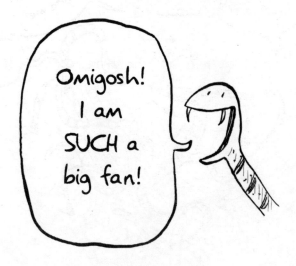

"R-Really...?" stammered Julius.

"Tell him Annie. Tell him I'm a big fan!"

"He's a big fan! In fact we're BOTH big fans! Although Tybalt here has seen more of your fights in Rome than I have."

"It's AMAZING to see you so close up!" gushed Tybalt. "You're normally so tiny and far away!"

"Oh, well," said Julius, getting all bashful, "I do hope I'm not a disappointment." He brushed his mane with his hoof.

"Sorry to be embarrassing," said Annie, "but can we have your hoofprint?"

Before Julius could answer, their sack suddenly jolted hard and Julius and the snakes were thrown from one end to the other.

And with a great thud, they landed on very hard ground.

Outside the bag, Julius could hear a frantic voice.

"PLEASE BE ALIVE! PLEASE BE ALIVE! I'VE BEEN SUCH AN IDIOT!"

With a great RIP, the top of the sack was pulled open and Julius and the two snakes flopped onto the grass.

Julius looked up to see his brother Brutus. "Yes, you HAVE been an idiot," he said.

"YOU'RE ALIVE!!" screamed Brutus. "The snakes didn't kill you!"

"Big fans of mine, apparently!" said Julius.

Brutus gave Julius a big hug. "I'm so sorry, Julius. Once I saw what they were going to do to you, I knew those Romans were RASCALS, just like you said!"

Julius let out a great big sigh. "So you didn't work that out after spending time with that rotter Victorious?"

"OOH no," said Brutus. "He was a RIGHT laugh! We've promised to keep in touch and everything. HATED you though. You proper upset him by beating him in front of thousands of people."

"He deserved it, the weasel," said Julius.

"I can't believe how much you've changed, Julius!" said Brutus. "Mum would be SO proud of you!"

Suddenly, something caught Brutus's eye. On the horizon he spotted a chariot coming over the hill.

"'Ere, Julius, am I going mad, or is that a giraffe on the back of that chariot?"

"RUFUS!" cried Julius. "And wait, that's Lucia holding the reins!"

Julius dashed out and waved frantically at the chariot. "LUCIA! WE'RE HERE!!"

"AMAZING!" cried Julius. "Where did you get the chariot?"

"These guys lent it to me!" said Lucia.

"Pericles, Berta and Douglas followed us all the way up to the wall, gathering warriors as they went!"

"LEAD THEM?!" Julius balked. "I didn't say I'd LEAD them, did I? I thought we'd just *work* together!"

A great chorus of swords thumping against wooden shields reverberated across the valley.

"You try telling THEM that!" chuckled Lucia.

Another chariot raced over, this time carrying Cornelius, Milus, Felix and Pliny.

"Sounds like you've made a name for yourself HERE too, zebra!" laughed Pliny.

CHAPTER TWENTY-TWO
BROTHERS IN ARMS

Julius and the army of Britons approached the Roman fort.

"How many of us are there?" asked Julius.

"About two thousand," replied Lucia.

"EXCELLENT! There's only a hundred of them, this will be easy."

Hadrian stood on the fort battlements.

Lay down your arms, zebra, and I will spare you and your friends!

"Did someone say something?" Julius asked Brutus. "I couldn't quite hear over the ROAR of my ENORMOUS ARMY." He thrust his hoof in the air and the horde of Britons charged against the fort.

The wooden gates crashed open like rotten firewood as the barbarians poured into the courtyard.

"They're running away like big chickens!" cried Brutus, as every last Roman soldier ran for their lives.

"Victory is OURS!" yelled Julius.

In the distance, Julius spotted Hadrian and Septimus speeding off on the Emperor's golden chariot.

Julius plopped to the ground, exhausted. "They'll be back, and in greater numbers," he wheezed.

"Aye," rasped a familiar voice. "And we'll be *waiting* for them."

"DOUGLAS!" cried Julius, leaping up. He grabbed him by the hoof. "Thank you for trusting me!"

"You've given us hope, zebra. Let's see if we can't kick these cockroaches out FOR EVER!"

Julius turned to his friends. "And we're FREE!!! We're ACTUALLY FREE!"

"But what about the other animal gladiators?" said Brutus.

"What do you mean?" asked Julius.

"Hadrian is training DOZENS of captured animals from all around the Empire. Maybe we should set them free too?"

Julius looked at his brother. "What, you mean we should take on ROME ITSELF?"

"Maybe." Brutus grinned. "Or you could go back to that stinky lake and drink the pooey water. It's up to YOU!"

At Ludus Magnus, Rome's biggest gladiator school, home to the city's gladiator champions, the past few months had seen many changes. Most not welcome to the veteran fighters.

Julius Zebra's success had prompted Hadrian to demand MORE bestial gladiators, of all shapes and sizes. The more animal gladiators on show, the happier his citizens were, and the happier his citizens were, the happier Hadrian was too.

Except that not *all* the animals captured and put up for training were *happy* to become gladiators.

In fact, one particular recruit was proving to be extremely difficult to handle.

"It's no good Victorious," said the bumbling

dungeon master. "No matter what I do, I can't keep her quiet!"

Victorious threw down his scroll. "DO I HAVE TO DO EVERYTHING MYSELF?!" He stormed down to the school arena, where his disobedient pupil was chained to a training pole.

"By Jupiter's beard, Zebra, what will it take for you to BEHAVE yourself?!"

"You will free me from these chains and take me to my SONS," demanded the zebra.

Or you will feel the sharp end of my HOOF!

TO BE CONTINUED...

ROMAN NUMERALS

Hello readers! Julius has asked me and Felix to help explain the strange page numbers used throughout this book.

Instead of page numbers like 1, 2 and 3, you'll find V, X, I and various other letters, which are Roman numerals — just like the Romans used for counting!

Even an idiot like me can understand them. Hooray!

Here are the seven letters that represent all the Roman numerals.

Thankfully, you won't find the last two... This book is big enough as it is!

I = 1
V = 5
X = 10
L = 50
C = 100
D = 500
M = 1000

You simply add Roman numerals together to make different numbers:

II (1 + 1) = 2
VIII (5 + 1 + 1 + 1) = 8
CLI (100 + 50 + 1) = 151

That seems easy enough! I'm off to collect some rocks.

WAIT! We're not finished! There are two basic things you need to know to be able to count Roman numerals!

Oh?

1: YOU WILL NEVER FIND MORE THAN THREE OF THE SAME ROMAN NUMERALS IN A ROW. 3 is written as III, but 4 is not IIII.

But hold on, how do you write 4 then?

My brain hurts!

2: WHEN A SMALLER NUMERAL COMES BEFORE A LARGER NUMERAL, TAKE AWAY THE VALUE OF THE SMALLER NUMERAL FROM THE BIGGER ONE TO WORK OUT THE NUMBER.

So 9 is IX?

Yes! You can remember it like this: 1 before 10 is 9.

To summarise: always read Roman numerals from left to right, adding up as you go along. If a larger numeral comes before a smaller or equal numeral, add them together. But if a smaller numeral comes before a larger numeral, take away the value of the smaller numeral from the bigger one before moving on to the next letter in the row.

If there is a next letter, of course!

Here's some to help you along!

1	I	10	X	50	L
2	II	11	XI	60	LX
3	III	12	XII	70	LXX
4	IV	13	XIII	80	LXXX
5	V	14	XIV	90	XC
6	VI	15	XV	100	C
7	VII	20	XX	200	CC
8	VIII	30	XXX		
9	IX	40	XL		

GARY'S FACTS:
WHAT THE ROMANS BROUGHT TO BRITAIN

ADVERTISING

We are bombarded by advertising at every turn these days and life wasn't so different in Roman Britain. The Romans would stick up posters for political messages, social events and, of course, sports events. No doubt Julius had his beautiful face drawn on such a poster!

APPLES AND PEARS

Often used by the Romans to sweeten recipes. Very popular with Cockney Londoners today, especially those who have staircases.

BATHS

Washing and gossiping were two of Rome's favourite things, which is why their baths were so popular. Widely introduced throughout Britain, the bath was such a hit that they even named a city after it! Toilets were just as popular with Romans, so I think we got off lightly there.

CALENDAR

Romans loved their calendars and our current Gregorian calendar is a direct descendant of the old Roman calendar and Julius Caesar's Julian calendar. They gave us most of our months,

GARY'S FACTS

including September (Latin *Septem*, meaning seven), October (Latin *Octo*, meaning eight), November (Latin *Novem*, meaning nine) and December (Latin *Decem*, meaning ten). We've added a couple of months to our calendar since, so those names don't make much sense now!

CARROTS

Originally came in red, black, yellow and white, as well as the familiar orange. Romans found them useful for medicine and for feeding all the rabbits that had recently turned up. (*See*: *Rabbits*)

CATS

Brought over as mascots by the Roman Army, domestic cats were also revered as gods of liberty. This meant they could come and go as they pleased, a privilege unchanged for the last 2000 years.

CEMENT

Being great engineers, the Romans used copious amounts of cement to construct their statues and buildings, plenty of which survives today. Workers even added volcanic ash to the mixture which, when left in water, would set as hard as rock. Whether Roman construction workers were also behind the origin of "builder's bum" is not so clear.

CENTRAL HEATING

Villas and baths were kept warm and cosy for chilly Romans by the circulation of warm air pumped up through holes in the floor and walls, via a furnace tended by slaves. The warm air vents were also greatly appreciated by lazy cats.

FLUSHING TOILETS

Thanks to their great ingenuity and love of cleanliness, Romans introduced continuously flowing water to their latrines. Toilets were communal, so you could sit and merrily chat with your mates as you did your "business".

LANGUAGE

The Roman language of Latin still permeates modern English to this day. Initially adopted by the aristocracy for posh documents, people of all classes now use Latin phrases *ad infinitum*. (See what I did there?)

GARY'S FACTS

LAW AND ORDER

Run much like an army, the Romans introduced the world's first organised police force throughout their Empire.

PAVED STREETS

The Romans built the first towns in Britain, introducing rigid grid networks of paved streets adorned with big stone buildings. The Britons had never seen anything quite like it!

PEAS

Originally brought over by the Romans from the Middle East, peas are now an important staple of the British Sunday roast. Not so great on toast (believe me, I've tried).

RABBITS

Rabbits were first domesticated by the Romans, who bred them for their meat, fur and wool. And also because they were cute, with jolly little faces. Probably.

STINGING NETTLES

Used by Romans for treating sore muscles and also for keeping legs warm by slapping them against the skin. Nowadays sold as soup in posh supermarkets.

STRAIGHT ROADS

Muddy, twisty-turny roads were OUT, straight stone roads were IN – all 10,000 miles of them. The Romans made their roads straight so that their marching army could invade your rebellious village even quicker. Hooray!

TURNIPS

Widely used by Romans as food for livestock during the cold winter months. Wow, eating turnips on a cold, wet day, standing in a muddy field: sheep and cows always knew how to have a good time.

WINE

Water was very unsafe to drink 2000 years ago, so Romans drank wine instead. Wine was so popular with the Romans that they drank 100 million litres a year in the city of Rome alone! In Britain everyone drank cheap beer, but the Romans hated the stuff, so they stuck to their wine.

Green and sparkly.

Rock with grass
growing out of it.

Coughed up
by a duck.

Piece of the
Pyramid of Giza.

Almost like bacon.

Nose fallen
off a statue.

Looks like the Moon.

Lucky stone.
(My second one,
lost the first one.)

Looks a bit like Julius.

Found under my bed.

Street cobblestone.

Reminds me of home.

ROCK COLLECTION

Identical stones.

Dropped from my ear.

Amber with fly inside.

Stone from
Londinium river.

From the race track at
the Circus Maximus.

Volcanic sponge.

Actually floats.

Emperor Nero's
favourite rock
(Replica).

Fell off the Colosseum.

Smallest stone in
the world.

Old stone tooth.

From Hadrian's garden.

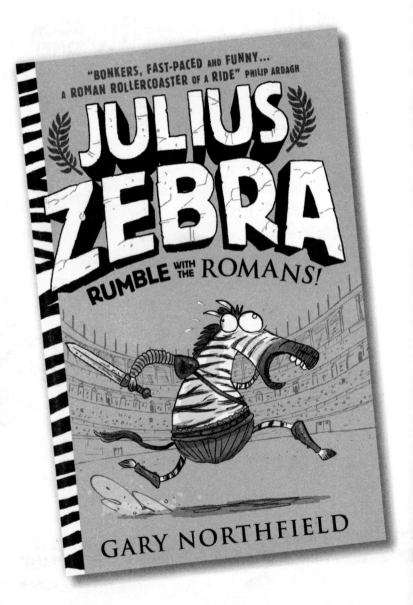

THEN GET
RUMBLING WITH THE ROMANS
IN JULIUS ZEBRA BOOK ONE!

Julius Zebra

So, you think you know
about ZEBRAS, do you?
They're handsome, eat lots of grass,
and um ... are always getting eaten by lions.
Let's face it, they're a little
bit boring and stupid, too. Oi!

But a tussle with a grumpy
gladiator can soon change a zebra...
So cheer on our stripy hero, Julius, as he
scraps for survival in history's deadliest theatre:

THE COLOSSEUM!

JUST DON'T CALL HIM A HORSE!

(or Debra...)

Gary Northfield has been writing and drawing comics since 2002. He is most famous for Derek the Sheep, a comic strip that appeared in *The Beano*. Gary has also created comics for *National Geographic Kids* magazine, *The Phoenix*, *The Dandy*, *The DFC*, *Horrible Histories* magazine, *Horrible Science* magazine and *The Magical World of Roald Dahl*. As well as the Julius Zebra books, Gary has published *The Terrible Tales of the Teenytinysaurs!* with Walker Books and *Gary's Garden* (nominated for the British Comic Awards) with David Fickling Books. One of Gary's favourite subjects is animals and their jolly lives, and he often wonders what they think about the world in which they live. Find Gary online at www.garynorthfield.com and on Twitter and Instagram as @gnorthfield.